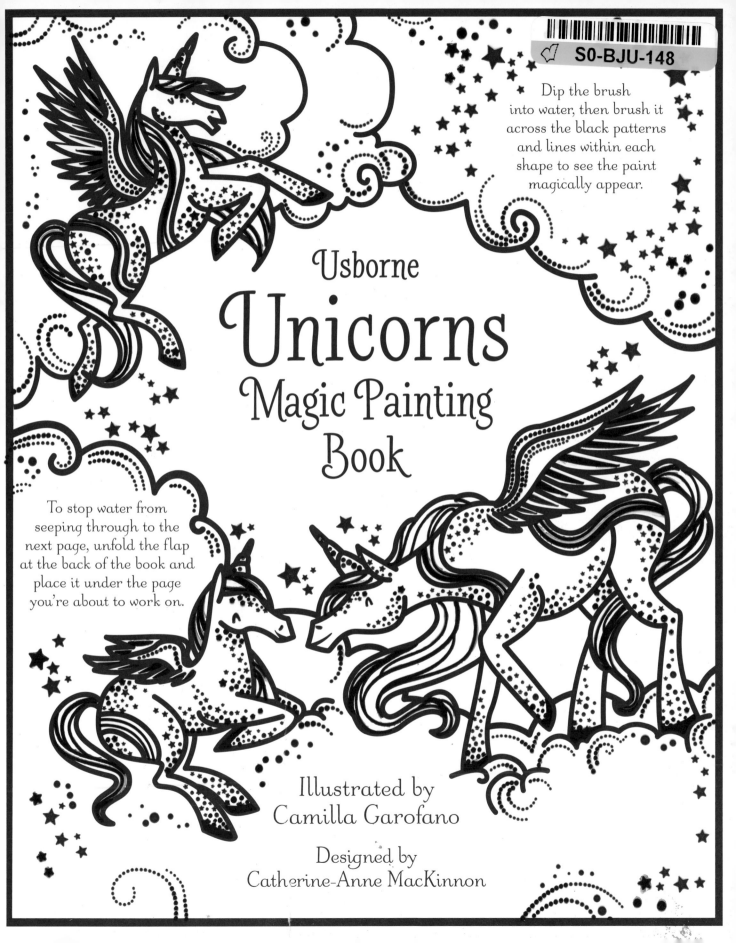

Dip the brush
into water, then brush it
across the black patterns
and lines within each
shape to see the paint
magically appear.

Usborne
Unicorns
Magic Painting
Book

To stop water from
seeping through to the
next page, unfold the flap
at the back of the book and
place it under the page
you're about to work on.

Illustrated by
Camilla Garofano

Designed by
Catherine-Anne MacKinnon